For my husband, Daniel, and the two
other creatures in our house—E.J.
For Marta, Cliff, and Ella Ania—T.B.

Text copyright © 2001 by Emily Jenkins

Pictures copyright © 2001 by Tomek Bogacki

All rights reserved

Distributed in Canada by Douglas & McIntyre Publishing Group

Printed in May 2011 in China by South China Printing Co. Ltd.,

Dongguan City, Guangdong Province

First edition, 2001

Sunburst edition, 2005

10 9 8 7 6

Library of Congress Cataloging-in-Publication Data

Jenkins, Emily, 1970–

    Five creatures / Emily Jenkins; pictures by Tomek Bogacki.

      p. cm.

    Summary: In words and pictures, a girl describes the three humans and two cats that

live in her house, and details some of the traits that they share.

    ISBN: 978-0-374-42328-5 (pbk.)

    [1. Family life–Fiction. 2. Cats–Fiction.] I. Bogacki, Tomasz, ill. II. Title.

PZ7.J4134 Fi 2001

[E]–dc21

                                                                                    00-28771

FIVE CREATURES

Emily Jenkins

Pictures by Tomek Bogacki

A Sunburst Book

Farrar, Straus and Giroux

Five creatures live in our house.

Three humans, and two cats.

Three short, and two tall.
Four grownups, and one child. (That's me!)

Three with orange hair, and two with gray.

Two with long hair, three with short.

Four who like to eat fish.

Three who like to drink milk, one who's allergic, and one who has it only in coffee.

Two who like to eat mice.

Only one who likes to eat beets.

Three who sleep in my bed.

Three who don't like taking baths.

Three who can button buttons.

Four who can open cupboards.

Four who can get up on the high stools.

One who can crawl under the fridge.

One who sings loud late at night.

And one who sings in the morning.

Three who nap with the Sunday newspaper.

Two who can read, and one who is learning.

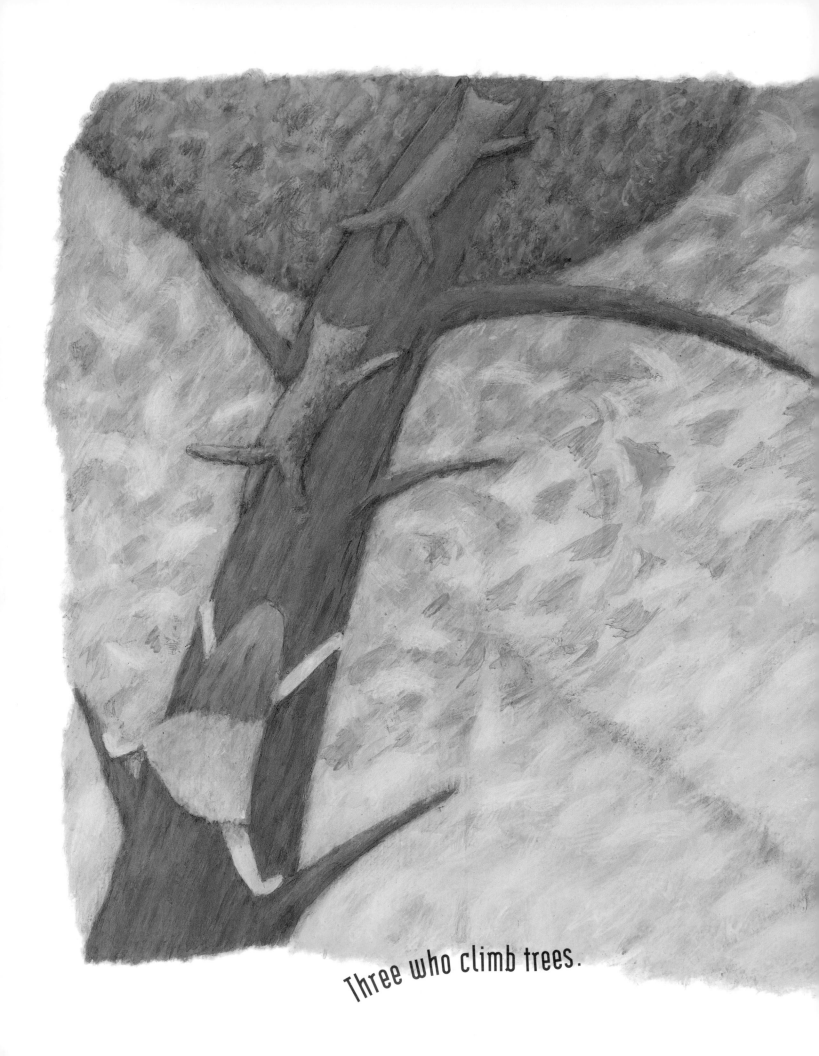

Three who climb trees.

And two who can't always get down.

Five who love birds . . .

but not all in the same way.

Three who like to hide in boxes.

Four who have a knack with yarn.

Two who lick each other.

Five who kiss each other.

And five who sit together in the evening by the fire.